# MR. BIRTHDAY

Roger Hargreaves

Original concept by
**Roger Hargreaves**

Written and illustrated by
**Adam Hargreaves**

EGMONT

The very best thing about birthdays, as far as Mr Birthday is concerned, is birthday parties.

Cards are nice, presents are good, but parties are great.

Mr Birthday likes birthday parties so much that he is never without his party hat!

And Mr Birthday is very good at organising birthday parties. He likes to make sure that everyone he knows has a party on their birthday.

In just the last three weeks, he has organised a party with two cakes for Mr Greedy.

A party with silly hats for Mr Silly because …

… Mr Silly is silly!

And a party with no balloons for Mr Jelly because
Mr Jelly is scared of balloons …

… in case they go POP!

This week, Mr Birthday organised a very happy birthday party for Mr Happy.

He invited all of Mr Happy's friends, including Little Miss Sunshine, Mr Funny, Little Miss Lucky and Mr Bump.

Mr Birthday put up lots of balloons and a big banner saying **"Happy Birthday, Mr Happy!"**

And he organised fun party games for everyone to play.

Happy Birthday, Mr Happy!

Little Miss Lucky won pass the parcel.

And then she won pin the tail on the donkey.

She is not called Little Miss Lucky for nothing!

It was difficult to know who won musical chairs because Mr Bump kept knocking over the chairs.

After the party games, Mr Birthday brought in a huge birthday cake. Mr Happy smiled an extra wide smile and blew out all the candles in one go!

Then they all ate a feast of birthday cake, jam sandwiches, jelly and ice-cream.

Everyone had a wonderful time.

When the party had finished, Mr Happy thanked Mr Birthday.

"We mustn't forget that extra special birthday next week," added Mr Happy with a wink, as he said goodbye.

Mr Birthday racked his brains as he walked home.

"I wonder whose birthday Mr Happy was talking about," he puzzled.

But try as he might, no one came to mind.

He looked in his diary when he reached home, but there was no one's birthday written in for the next week.

"Mr Happy must have got it wrong," he reassured himself as he got into bed.

But the next day, Mr Birthday kept overhearing things that seemed to suggest there really was a very important birthday coming up.

He passed Mr Worry in the street.

"Oh my! Oh gosh! What ever am I going to buy as a present for next week?" muttered Mr Worry to himself. "What a worry!"

He overheard Mr Forgetful who was repeating,
"I must not forget the party next week, I must not
forget the party next week, I must not forget the party
next week," over and over to himself.

"I must not forget the ..." he said and stopped
mid-sentence. Then he looked at his hand,
"... the party! I must not forget the party next week."

Poor Mr Birthday was distraught. How could there
be a birthday, and a birthday party, he knew
nothing about?

The following day, he decided that he would just have to go and ask Mr Happy.

Mr Happy smiled an even wider smile than usual when Mr Birthday admitted that he did not have a clue whose birthday they were all talking about.

"If you come back at 3 o'clock on Tuesday then I will tell you whose birthday it is," said Mr Happy.

By Tuesday, Mr Birthday was very, very curious.

Have you guessed whose birthday it is yet?

Mr Birthday turned up at Mr Happy's house at 3 o'clock on the dot.

"You have got to tell me now!" burst out Mr Birthday, when Mr Happy opened the door.

"With pleasure," grinned Mr Happy. "It is …"

"… your birthday!"

**"Happy birthday, Mr Birthday!"** cried all
of Mr Birthday's friends.

Mr Birthday blushed, "How silly of me!" he said.